Beginners
Are
Brave

Redleaf Lane

WRITTEN BY
Rachel Robertson

ILLUSTRATED BY
Faryn Hughes

To my parents, Tom and Catherine, who have always given me the support and encouragement I needed, no matter what I was trying.

—*Rachel*

To my grandfathers Mike and Bob. Thank you for all the joyful memories.

—*Faryn*

Published by Redleaf Lane
An imprint of Redleaf Press
10 Yorkton Court
Saint Paul, MN 55117
www.redleafpress.org

Text © 2020 by Rachel Robertson
Illustration © 2020 by Redleaf Press

First edition 2020
Senior editor: Heidi Hogg
Managing editor: Douglas Schmitz
Art director: Renee Hammes
Book jacket and interior design: Michelle Lee Lagerroos
Main body text set in Hero New

Printed in East Peoria, Illinois
27 26 25 24 23 22 21 20   1 2 3 4 5 6 7 8

Library of Congress Cataloging-in-Publication Data

Names: Robertson, Rachel, author. | Hughes, Faryn, illustrator.
Title: Beginners are brave / written by Rachel Robertson ; illustrated by Faryn
    Hughes.
Description: First Edition. | Saint Paul, MN : Redleaf Press, [2020] |
    Audience: Age: 3-8.
Identifiers: LCCN 2018059778 (print) | LCCN 2019011259 (ebook) | ISBN
    9781605546018 (e-book) | ISBN 9781605546001 (hardcover : alk. paper)
Subjects: LCSH: Resilience (Personality trait)--Juvenile literature.
Classification: LCC BF698.35.R47 (ebook) | LCC BF698.35.R47 R623 2019 (print)
    | DDC 155.2/4--dc23
LC record available at https://lccn.loc.gov/2018059778

Tommy was good at almost everything.

He was awesome at riding his bike without training wheels.

He was terrific at teaching his dog, Moxie, new tricks.

He was stupendous at spelling
seven-letter words like
kumquat and *acrobat*.

And he was the very, very best at making backyard blanket forts.

Tommy had been good at these things for as long as he could remember.

But there was **one thing** Tommy had forgotten how to do . . .

He'd forgotten
how to try
new things.

But he couldn't avoid trying new things **forever,** could he? He was just a kid after all and still needed to learn a few things, like how to drive a car and how to shave a mustache.

In fact, Tommy had something he secretly wanted to learn someday.

Every evening, Tommy lay on the rug beside his grandfather's chair. As his grandpa tapped his toes to his favorite tunes, Tommy dreamed of being a **world-famous tuba player.**

One night, Tommy's grandpa noticed Tommy's toes—*tap tap*—and asked, "Do you want to learn to play?"

"Not really," Tommy said glumly—even though he actually did.

You see, even more than wanting to learn to play the tuba, Tommy didn't want to make any mistakes. He didn't want to be a beginner. Being a beginner felt **too scary.**

So Tommy kept on riding his bicycle without training wheels, teaching his dog new tricks, spelling seven-letter words like **pizzazz** and **Frisbee**, and making backyard blanket forts.

Until one day, while out for a walk with Moxie, Tommy and his grandpa strolled past a music store. "Let's go in," Grandpa suggested.

Tommy's eyes searched the room for the tubas.

He spotted a row of them—shiny in their stands.

"Want to take a closer look?" his grandpa asked.

Tommy could feel his fingers twitching to press the cool brass keys. He could almost see himself on stage between the trumpet players and the saxophone players.

When Grandpa interrupted his daydream, Tommy noticed he was holding a large black case. "We're renting one that's close to your size," Grandpa grinned. "It might be fun."

Tommy's stomach flipped and flopped. He was a little excited and a lot nervous.

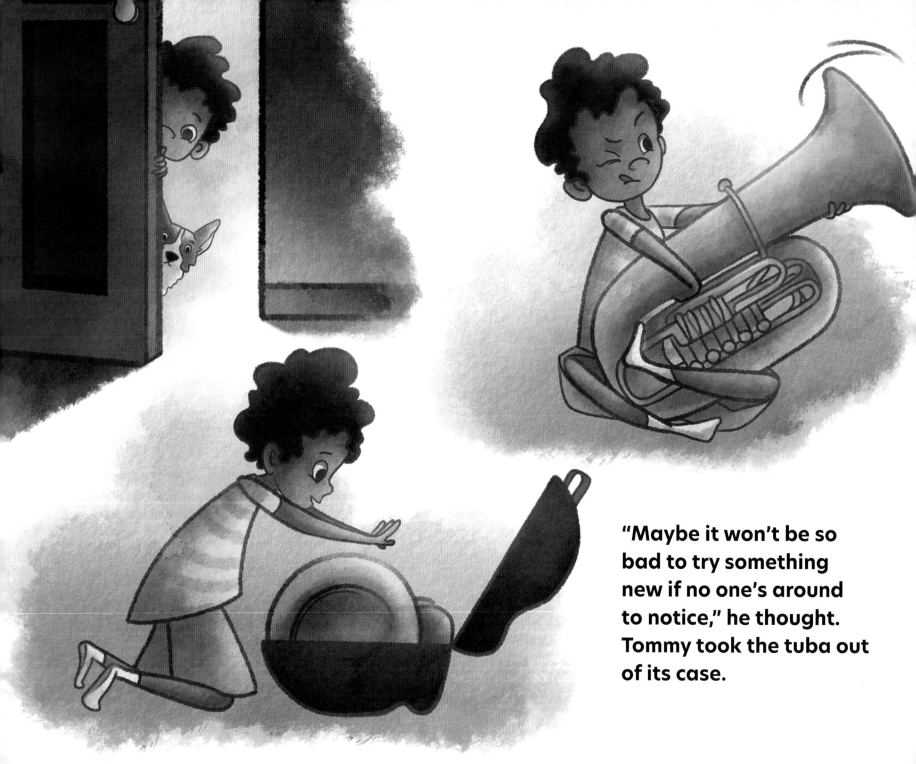

"Maybe it won't be so bad to try something new if no one's around to notice," he thought. Tommy took the tuba out of its case.

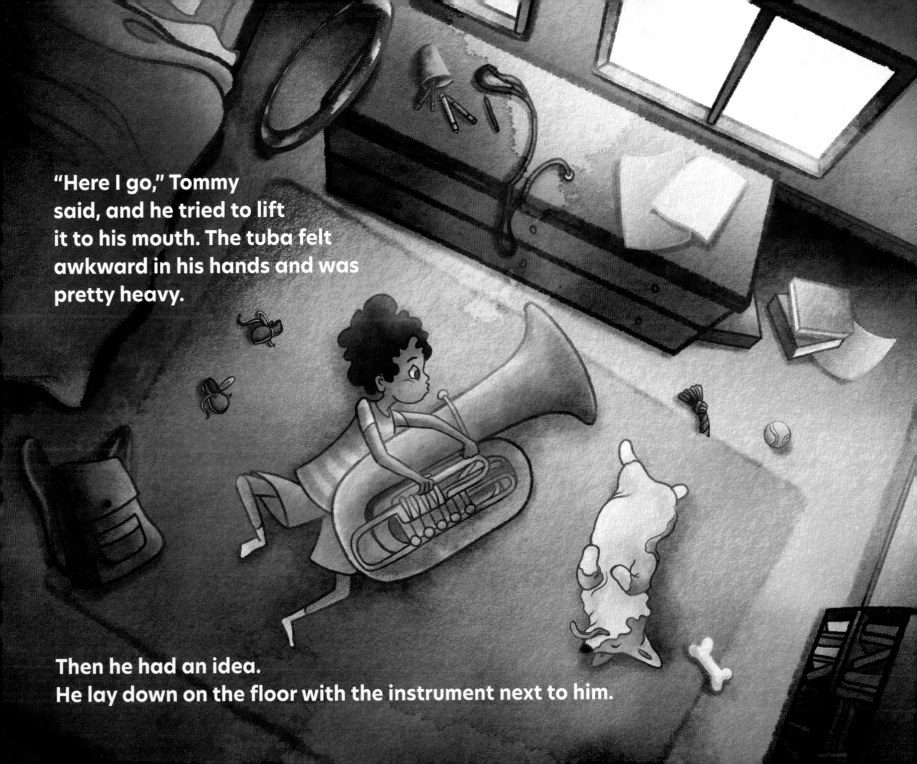

"Here I go," Tommy said, and he tried to lift it to his mouth. The tuba felt awkward in his hands and was pretty heavy.

Then he had an idea.
He lay down on the floor with the instrument next to him.

He put his lips to the mouthpiece. He took a deep breath.
He imagined playing the tuba so loud that it would sound like a
foghorn! He squeezed his eyes shut and blew with all his might.

Nothing.

He tried again.

Still nothing.

"It's too hard! I just
can't do it!"
he thought.
Tommy shoved
the tuba
back in its case.

On the walk to school, Grandpa asked how tuba practice was going.

"Not so good," Tommy mumbled.

"You know, Tommy," Grandpa said. "It's okay to be frustrated and make mistakes. That's how you learn. **You're brave to be a beginner."**

Tommy thought about what his grandpa said while he was at school and took a few deep breaths. He was ready to try again.

BELIEVE in YOURSELF

MISTAKES ARE OK! MISTAKES help us GROW

BRING ON THE CHALLENGE

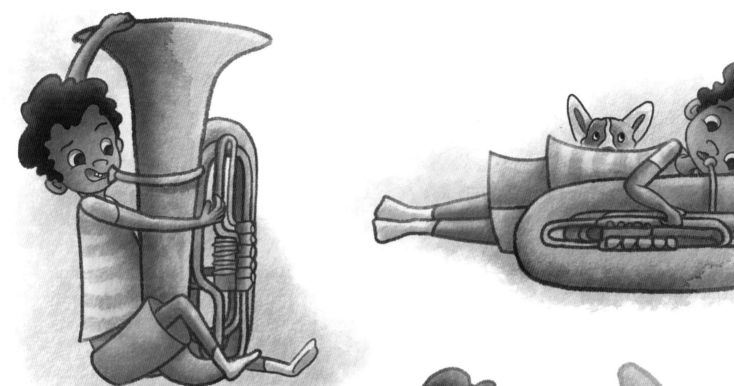

He took the tuba out of its case and tried putting his lips in different positions on the mouthpiece. He felt a little silly, but finally the tuba muttered, **"Blurp."**

BLURP

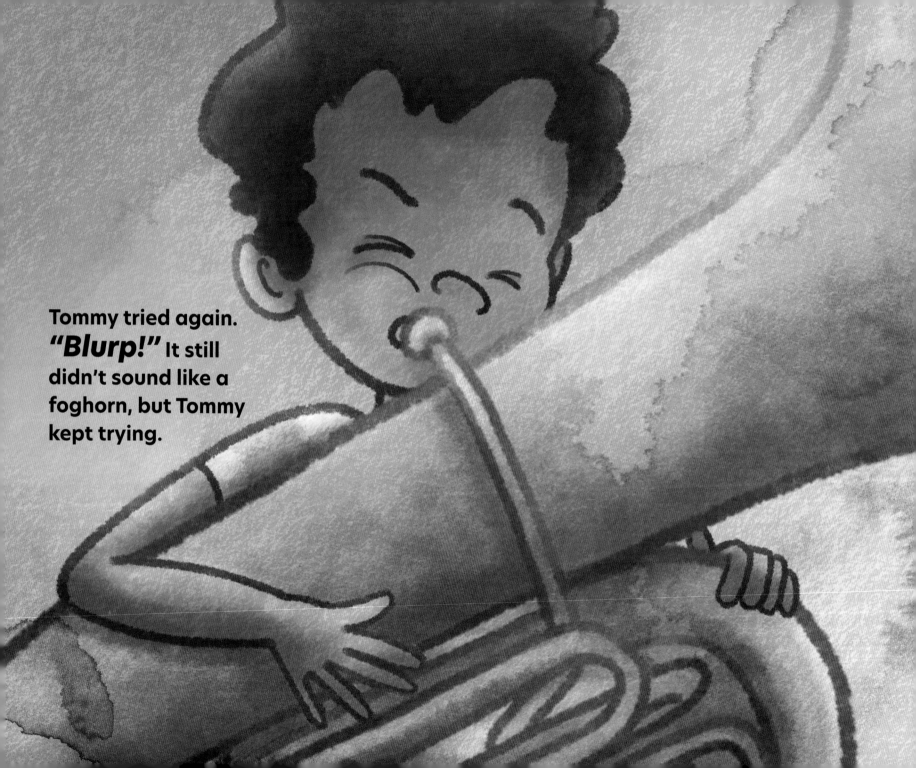

Tommy tried again. **"*Blurp!*"** It still didn't sound like a foghorn, but Tommy kept trying.

Pretty soon his small sounds turned into big sounds. And his **burrumpphhing** and **baaaoomming** could be heard down the block.

**And guess what all that trying did?
It turned Tommy into a tuba player!**

(According to Moxie, he still has a way to go before
he becomes a virtuoso).

In fact, he was already dreaming about becoming a juggling unicyclist.

A Note to Readers

Being a beginner is brave *because it can feel very hard*. As children develop increasingly complex emotions, they can be more hesitant. As they mature, "It's too hard" or "I can't" become more frequent phrases. But with time and opportunity, children often persist through the awkward beginner phase and find out that most often "they can"!

Being a beginner is also brave *because it is very important*. Children's efforts lead to a growth mind-set (the belief that they can learn and change) and personal agency (a set of skills that include goal setting, planning, and making choices). With these abilities, children are much more likely to have school, career, and life happiness and success.

Unfortunately, more and more children are expressing reluctance to try new things. Plentiful cultural messages imply that being a beginner is risky and that being average at something should be avoided.

What can you do?

- Consider yourself a role model and show children your willingness to try.
- Give children extensive unstructured playtime. Play is the perfect time to try, fail, and try again.
- Reinforce the message that mistakes are okay and that gaining new skills is a messy process.
- Always make failing safe. If children are scared to fail or do something wrong, they will avoid trying.
- Focus on effort over outcome. Enjoy the process of learning over the product.
- Help children discover rather than giving them the answers or taking over if they're slow. Instead, suggest an idea ("What if . . .?") or get something started (for example, helping with the first loop on a shoelace).
- When children say, "I can't" or "I'm not good at . . ." add the word "yet" to the end of that statement.

I hope you will apply the strategies in this book and inspire children to become brave beginners.